This Candlewick book belongs to:

_____

_____

_____

Thirtieth anniversary edition 2014

The Library of Congress has cataloged
the first Candlewick Press hardcover edition as follows:
Browne, Anthony.
Gorilla / Anthony Browne. —1st Candlewick Press ed.
p.   cm.
Reprint. Originally published: New York : Knopf, 1983.
Summary: Neglected by her busy father, a lonely young girl receives a toy gorilla for her birthday
and together they take a miraculous trip to the zoo.
ISBN 978-0-7636-1813-1 (first Candlewick hardcover)
[1. Gorilla—Fiction. 2. Fathers and daughters—Fiction.] I. Title.
PZ7.B81984 Go 2002
[E]—dc21   2001043756

ISBN 978-0-7636-7222-5 (thirtieth anniversary hardcover)
ISBN 978-0-7636-7366-6 (paperback)

14 15 16 17 18 SWT 10 9 8 7 6 5 4 3 2

Printed in Dongguan, Guangdong, China

This book was typeset in Palatino.
The illustrations were done in watercolor.

Candlewick Press
99 Dover Street
Somerville, Massachusetts 02144

visit us at www.candlewick.com

ANTHONY BROWNE
GORILLA

CANDLEWICK PRESS

Hannah loved gorillas. She read books about gorillas, she watched gorillas on television, and she drew pictures of gorillas. But she had never seen a real gorilla.

Her father didn't have time to take her to see one at the zoo. He didn't have time for anything.

He went to work every day before Hannah went to school, and in the evening he worked at home.

When Hannah asked him a question, he would say, "Not now. I'm busy. Maybe tomorrow."

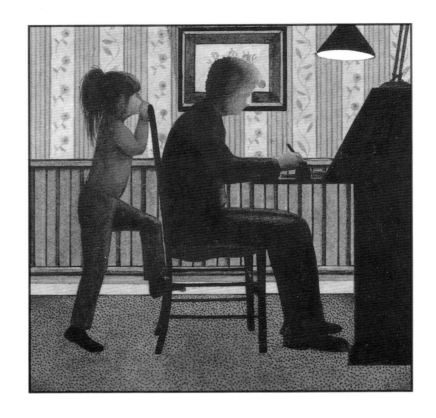

But the next day he was always too busy.
"Not now. Maybe on the weekend," he would say.

But on the weekend he was always too tired.
They never did anything together.

The night before her birthday, Hannah went to bed tingling with excitement — she had asked her father for a gorilla!

In the middle of the night, Hannah woke up and saw a very small parcel at the foot of the bed. It *was* a gorilla, but it was just a toy.

Hannah threw the gorilla into a corner with her
other toys and went back to sleep.

In the night something amazing happened.

Hannah was frightened. "Don't be frightened, Hannah," said the gorilla, "I won't hurt you. I just wondered if you'd like to go to the zoo."
The gorilla had such a nice smile that Hannah wasn't afraid.
"I'd love to," she said.

They both crept downstairs, and Hannah put on her coat. The gorilla put on her father's hat and coat. "A perfect fit," he whispered.

They opened the front door and went outside.

"Come on then, Hannah," said the gorilla, and he gently lifted her up. Then they were off, swinging through the trees toward the zoo.

When they arrived at the zoo it was closed, and there was
a high wall all around. "Never mind," said the gorilla.
"Up and over!"

They went straight to the primates. Hannah was thrilled.
So many gorillas!

The gorilla took Hannah to see the orangutan and a chimpanzee.
She thought they were beautiful. But sad.

"What would you like to do now?" the gorilla asked.

"I'd love to go to the movies," said Hannah.

So they did.

Afterward they walked down the street together. "That was wonderful," said Hannah, "but I'm hungry now."

"OK," said the gorilla. "We'll eat."

"Time for home?" asked the gorilla.
  Hannah nodded, a bit sleepily.

They danced on the lawn. Hannah had never been so happy.

"You better go in now, Hannah," said the gorilla. "See you tomorrow."

"Really?" asked Hannah.

The gorilla nodded and smiled.

The next morning Hannah woke up and saw the toy gorilla. She smiled.

Hannah rushed downstairs to tell her father what had happened.

"Happy birthday, love," he said. "Do you want to go to the zoo?"
Hannah looked at him.

She was very happy.